Carol screamed for help. My mother charged to the other side of the room and blocked the door. Pigsy spun around just in time and headed back in my direction. He was trailing lace and ribbons behind him.

No one could catch him. Mom was running in one direction. The seamstress and her assistant were running in the other direction. The dining room looked like a snow storm of material and lace. Carol was stomping her feet and squealing almost as much as the pig. I would have laughed if the grown-ups hadn't been so serious.

"Do something, Sherri!" Carol yelled. "Do something before my whole wedding is ruined!"

My Sister, The Pig, And Me

by Cindy Savage

cover art by Gabriel
inside illustration by Estella Hickman

For Lisa Marie,
who will soon be as adventuresome as P.W.

Published by Willowisp Press, Inc.
10100 SBF Drive, Pinellas Park, Florida 34666

Copyright © 1992 by Cindy Savage
Covers and illustrations copyright © 1992 by Willowisp Press, Inc.

Printed in the United States of America

2 4 6 8 10 9 7 5 3 1

ISBN 0-87406-638-7

One

"THIS is going to be the greatest job I've had since I started my pet-sitting business last summer!" I said to Lynn, my best friend. We were walking through Grove Park on Friday afternoon. It was the beginning of spring break.

Lynn just shook her head. "Sherri Waverly," she said, "I still can't believe you're actually going to take care of a pig! I wouldn't have any idea what to do with one!"

I smiled and reached down to pat Rusty on the head. Rusty is a reddish-brown cocker spaniel that I exercise every day for my neighbor, Mrs. Dapple. Rusty is the first pet I ever took care of for money. You could say that Rusty launched my pet-sitting career. But more about that later.

"Pigsy Wigsy isn't exactly a *regular* pig," I told Lynn as we turned down a path leading through the park's rose garden. "He's a Vietnamese potbellied pig. Potbellied pigs are miniature pigs, and they're getting popular as pets. Mrs. Pinkston told me that real hogs sometimes weigh as much as 1,000 pounds, but Pigsy only weighs 35 pounds. He's a *house* pig."

Lynn's blue eyes grew wide. She blew her brown bangs off her forehead. "You mean he lives *in* the house? My mother would have a fit! She even hates my goldfish, and I clean his bowl every day."

"Whew! I'm glad my mom and dad aren't that way," I said. "I would have lost a lot of pet-sitting jobs if they were. Remember that time I kept Mr. Robertson's cat for two weeks while he went on a business trip?"

"And don't forget the Kinks' python snake," Lynn added.

"That snake was really cool!" I said. "I hated to feed it mice, though. I felt so sorry for them."

"That's life in the jungle, I guess," Lynn said with a giggle.

We left the rose garden and headed for the duck pond. Rusty pulled happily at his leash.

"Just thinking about a jungle reminds me of our house," I said. "It's just about as wild as a jungle right now. I never knew having my sister get married was going to be such a hassle."

Rusty suddenly became interested in a certain patch of grass. Lynn and I paused while he investigated.

"Why? What's going on?" Lynn asked.

I rolled my eyes. "What isn't going on is more like it," I said. "I wish Carol were like everyone else who goes to a church or a garden or someplace else to get married. But no, Carol is getting married right in our backyard. Not only do we have to clean the house and yard from top to bottom, but we're *making* all of the decorations and stuff."

"What about the food?"

"We're making that, too," I said. "Carol cooks part-time in a restaurant to help pay her way through this fancy chef's school she's been going to. And now that she's learning all this great stuff about gourmet cooking, she doesn't think she can trust anyone else to make the perfect food that she wants to serve. And as if that weren't enough, my mom is making all the bouquets and corsages and centerpieces. She's been the window dresser at Jared's Department Store for so long that my sister thought she'd be great at it."

"Well, I guess doing all the preparation stuff yourselves will save a pile of money," Lynn said.

"Yes, but it takes a lot of time," I grumbled. " I might as well be invisible. Since this whole wedding business started, everything is 'Carol this' and 'Carol that.' It's like I'm in the way."

"That's awful!"

"You're telling me! At first I thought having Carol's wedding at our house might be exciting. But now I'm not so sure."

"When is the wedding, anyway?" asked Lynn.

"A week from tomorrow," I said. "Carol and John are coming tonight, and they're going to stay for the whole week to get things ready."

"Maybe that will be better," Lynn reasoned. "There will be two extra pairs of hands."

I shrugged. "More likely, just two extra adults to boss me around."

"That doesn't sound like Carol or like John," Lynn said. "I thought you liked your sister and her fiancé."

I tugged on Rusty's leash. "I *do* like my sister," I said. "And I *do* like John. When Carol told me that she and John were getting married, I was really happy. John is great brother material, but..."

"But what?"

"But the last time Carol was here to work

10

out details for the wedding, she acted as if I were just a fly on the wall or something," I said. "I tried to make suggestions, and even Mom ignored me. Carol kept giving me dumb jobs to do to get me out of the way. I'm smart enough to do more than just take out the garbage."

"Plenty more," Lynn agreed. "Didn't your mom tell Carol that you even planted some of the flowers for the wedding in the backyard?"

"She told her, but Carol was too busy making lists to notice. She didn't even go out in the backyard to see. Instead, she sent me off to fold laundry."

"Sounds like she wanted you out of her hair," said Lynn. "I feel that way about my little sisters sometimes."

"Lynn! Your little sisters are only two and three years old! I'm ten! That's almost grown up! I mean, I know Carol hasn't been back home much in the past two years, but I'm not as little as she remembers me. I just want to help out."

Lynn shook her head. "I never have understood why you like to work around the house so much," she said. "I try to get out of every job I can."

"Maybe that's the difference between being the oldest in the family and the youngest in the family," I explained. "You hate your jobs because *everyone* expects you to do them. I like my jobs because *no one* expects me to do them. They're always surprised when I do something they don't think I'm old enough to do yet."

Rusty quit sniffing the grass and charged across a field. He yanked me along by his leash. Lynn and I laughed and ran after him.

Lynn and I have been best friends since kindergarten. We have a lot in common. We both have long brown hair and blue eyes, and both of us would rather be outdoors than indoors. What makes it even better is the fact that we live next door to each other.

When I decided to try pet-sitting for a business, it was Lynn who encouraged me the most. I think that's partly because her parents won't let her have a pet that does anything except swim in a bowl.

See, I'm too young to baby-sit, but people going away for vacations need someone responsible to come to their house and feed their animals. I water plants, too, if they need it. It all started when Mrs. Dapple got an afternoon job and couldn't take Rusty for his daily stroll. On our way home from school one day, Lynn and I spotted Rusty peeking through the fence. He looked so sad that I asked Mrs. Dapple if she would let me walk him. She said yes, and I really enjoyed it. Before long I was taking Rusty to the park almost every day after school.

Then one day Mrs. Dapple told me that she had to go on a trip for three days. She asked if I would be interested in feeding Rusty, too. She paid me and told the other neighbors what a good job I did. My pet-sitting business was born.

Since then I've taken care of dogs, cats,

snakes, frogs, fish, guinea pigs, goats, and once, even a horse. Lynn has been right there with me, getting her fill of the pets that her parents won't let her have. Maybe, I thought, we could become veterinarians together when we were old enough.

Lynn interrupted my daydreaming and said, "So, when Carol comes home, she makes you feel like a baby, and your parents treat you that way too?"

I nodded. "I don't know why everything changes when she walks in the door, but it does," I said. "Thank goodness I'll have Pigsy Wigsy to keep me company this week."

"Bringing home a pig is different than bringing home a dog," Lynn said as we walked out of the park. With Rusty leading the way, we turned onto our street. "With all the stuff that has to be done to get ready for the wedding, your parents might not appreciate a live-in pig right now."

"I doubt they'll even notice," I said. "They

haven't noticed me lately, so why should they notice a pig? But don't worry. I'm going to ask permission tonight at dinner. I always ask if I'm planning a pet-sitting job at the house. Mom and Dad will probably be glad that I have something to do to keep me out of their way."

Two

I looked around my room when I got home and sighed. Wedding favors were piled everywhere. Almonds ready to be tied in little snippets of white net had been set on the overstuffed chair in the corner of my room. I loved to curl up on the chair when I read, but now it looked like a pin cushion.

That wasn't all. There were tiny plastic swans stacked on my dresser. The swans would be stuffed with jelly beans, and satin ribbons would be tied around their necks. Rolls of the ribbon were beside the swans. And piled on my desk were bigger rolls of peach and white ribbon that would be turned into bows

17

for the backs of chairs.

It was a good thing that spring vacation had started because I sure wouldn't get any school work done.

My room wasn't the only room filled with wedding junk. As I walked out to the dining room for dinner I peeked into the other rooms. The den was full of paper plates, cups, napkins, punch bowls, and serving trays. The living room was piled with tablecloths, and the refrigerator was filled with hors d'oeuvre fixings.

Part of me minded all the clutter, but part of me didn't. I had to admit that when I wasn't being treated like a baby, the wedding preparation was pretty exciting. Who knew? Maybe now that the wedding was so close, Carol would relax and we'd have fun the way we used to when she lived at home. We could do things together, and when she was busy, I could play catch with John. Next to my dad, John's the best catch partner I've ever had.

"Sherri?" My mother called to me before I

rounded the corner. "Could you go into the den and bring out the regular napkins? I must have taken them in there by mistake. And Frisky needs to be let out."

"Sure, Mom," I said, turning back toward the den. I brought the napkins with me to the dining room, opened the package, and put them in the holder. It was almost time for dinner, and Mom's vegetable lasagna smelled great. Sniffing the air, I walked to the kitchen door and let our black cocker spaniel out onto the side yard.

"Good boy, Frisky. Keep your ears up!"

Frisky bounded out, then looked back hopefully.

"I'll come out and play with you after dinner," I called, and I went back inside. I jingled the bell on the cockatiel's cage as I passed by it. Cookoo gave a squawk which seems to be bird talk for just about anything.

"Anything else?" I asked Mom as I started to slip onto my chair at the table.

Mom and Dad were just sitting down too. "Uh-oh," said Mom. "I forgot the salt and pepper." She and Dad both started to get up.

"I'll get them," I said and headed into the kitchen. I really do like to help. After Carol moved out, my mom and dad started relying on me more. They were really proud of me when I started my pet-sitting business.

I set the salt and pepper shakers on the table and sat down. "The lasagna looks great," I said.

"It sure does," said Dad. He put some lasagna on each of our plates, and we all dug in. "How's our entrepreneur doing today?" he asked a minute later. Entrepreneur is a fancy word for someone who starts her own business.

"Just fine, Dad," I said, "and busy! It seems like everyone is going out of town at the same time. Before I took Rusty for his walk today I stopped by the Rolston house to get last-minute instructions for taking care of their two cats. Did I also tell you that Mrs. Hooper is leaving me in charge of her hermit crabs?"

"Just don't get in a pinch," Dad joked.

I rolled my eyes. "I doubt they'll even come out of their shells," I told him. "They're very shy."

"Didn't we see something about hermit crabs on that nature special the other night, Marge?" Dad asked.

"Huh?" Mom looked up from her plate. "Sorry, I didn't catch that."

Dad grinned at me. "Never mind. We're just talking about crabs."

"I'm not crabby," Mom protested. "I'm just preoccupied—busy, you know. There's a lot to do to get ready for a wedding."

"We know, dear," said Dad. "We're just teasing. You and Carol are doing a great job. In fact, Sherri and I are all yours for the next week. Just tell us what to do."

I swallowed a bite and said, "Yeah, Mom. When I'm not taking care of my animals, I can tie the almonds into the net bags. I can also put the ribbons on the swans."

"That's nice, Sherri, but I'm simply not ready to think about those table favors yet," said Mom. "Actually, I really can't get started on anything until Carol arrives. I need to finalize the last-minute arrangements with her. I mean, I don't even know if she wants two almonds or three almonds in the nets. Does she want them all tied with peach ribbon, or does she want half and half, peach and white?"

What was the big deal? I wondered. The almond favors would be pretty either way. Besides, the guests were just going to unwrap the nets and eat the almonds anyway.

I was more interested in getting permission to take care of Pigsy Wigsy for the week. Mrs. Pinkston was going to pay me double because Pigsy Wigsy—P.W. for short—was such an unusual pet. She inherited P.W. from an aunt less than two weeks ago and was getting used to him. But she told me there was still an awful lot she didn't know. She tried to put off her business trip to England so that she could stay home and learn more, but she wasn't able to.

I was more than happy to take the job. I love animals, and the idea of taking care of a pig sounded like fun. And it's usually no problem to get Mom and Dad to give me permission to bring pets home temporarily. When I started my business, they gave me just a few rules: Only work for people I know or they have met, and ask permission if I need to keep a pet at our house.

"So, Mom, Dad, I haven't told you yet about this other pet-sitting job I have starting tomorrow," I began.

"You're really doing well with your business," Mom said. I had the feeling she was still thinking about wedding details, but she glanced over and smiled at me. "How much money have you made so far?"

"Almost $50," I said proudly. "And this job is going to pay double what I usually make. I have to bring P.W. here, though."

"Really? Is it another snake?" Dad asked. "You know, I actually enjoyed having that python around. He was fascinating!"

"No, this isn't a snake, and it only eats vegetables," I said. "I'll bet you can't guess."

Dad had just opened his mouth to guess when the doorbell rang twice.

"Guess who's here!" Carol called from the front hallway.

"Already!" Mom exclaimed. "I didn't expect them in for another hour or so."

"I'd better go help with their bags," Dad said, getting up.

"And I'd better set two more places," Mom said, heading in the opposite direction.

I waited at the table for everyone to come back. I heard excited voices coming from the hall. Then Carol bustled into the kitchen. Her face was red from the wind and her blond hair was blown in every direction.

"Hi, Carol," I said.

"Hi, squirt!" she replied. "Are you all ready

for the wedding? How does your dress look?"

Squirt! I made a face and said, "I haven't seen the dress yet."

"What's that look for?" Carol asked. She smoothed her hair back from her face. Her hazel eyes looked at me curiously.

"Couldn't I just wear my jeans?" I begged. "You can sew on some peach lace."

Carol groaned. "No bridesmaid in the history of the world has ever worn jeans!" she said.

I doubted that, but I didn't say anything. At least Carol seemed to be in a better mood than the last time she came.

Carol looked at Mom who was coming out of the kitchen with two plates. "What's going on with Sherri's dress?" she asked, sitting down. "Is there some kind of problem?"

"No problem. The seamstress is coming tomorrow for a fitting," Mom said. "There was some problem at the shop. One of her assistants got the flu and she had to train someone new."

"So long as it's done on time, that's all that matters," Carol said. "It will be done on time, right?"

"As far as I know," said Mom.

"Where's John?" I asked, suddenly realizing that my future brother-in-law wasn't with Carol.

Carol pulled off her coat and draped it over the back of her chair. "You'll never believe this, but he has to go to a seminar for his work. It's some kind of training class or something, and he's not going to be here until next Friday!"

"But that's just one day before the wedding!" Mom said.

"What's John training for?" I asked.

"Rotten luck, huh?" Carol said to Mom, ignoring me. "I was really counting on him to help out with the last-minute details."

And I was counting on having someone around who wouldn't treat me like a piece of the furniture, I thought, just as disappointed. It was a good thing I'd have P.W to keep me company.

Thinking about P.W. reminded me that I still hadn't told my parents what type of animal I was bringing home for the week. I waited to see if there would be a break in the conversation.

"So, what about the flowers?" Carol asked as she dug into her lasagna.

"Uh... Mom?" I said, trying to be polite about interrupting. "Excuse me, but—"

"They'll be delivered on Wednesday," Mom said to Carol. "We'll just have to keep them refrigerated until the wedding."

"Uh, Mom?" I tried again.

"I think maybe we should rent an extra refrigerator for the week," Dad suggested. "Too many things need to be stored. What are you going to do with all of the pigs-in-blankets?"

"I've decided to use cheese in the centers of the blankets instead of hot dogs," Carol said.

"They'll still have to be refrigerated," Dad remarked.

"Speaking of pigs..." I began.

"We'll just put the hors d'oeuvres in the freezer until Friday night, Dad," Carol explained. "I'm more worried about having room for the flowers and keeping them looking fresh."

"Not to worry," Mom said. "I got the 'okay' to use the deli-refrigerator at Jared's for a couple of days. As we finish the flower arrangements and corsages, we'll take them over to Jared's for safekeeping. They'll be fine."

"That's great!" said Carol. "That's at least one thing I can almost relax about."

The phone rang and Dad left to grab it. Mom and Carol didn't miss a beat. They went back and forth about the flowers. Frisky started to bark up a storm outside. He was getting tired of waiting for me to play with him.

I couldn't hang around the dinner table forever, but it was looking more and more like I'd never get a chance to get a word in edgewise. Finally, I just blurted straight out what I wanted. "Mom," I said, "I need to keep Mrs.

Pinkston's potbellied pig here for the week while she goes to England. Is that okay?"

"What did you say, Sherri?" Mom asked. She had pushed her dinner plate away and was jotting notes on a piece of scratch paper.

Carol was craning her neck to watch everything Mom wrote down. She looked up briefly to grumble about Frisky's barking giving her a headache.

"I said that I need to bring P.W. here for the week. Is that all right with you?"

"What? Oh, sure, honey," said Mom. She waved a hand toward me and wrote down another note. "Just keep him out of mischief. And please, Sherri, go do something about Frisky."

"Right away," I said, "and thanks, Mom. I'll call Mrs. Pinkston and let her know everything is set!"

I expected Mom to ask more questions about P.W., but she and Carol were back to their wedding details. As I left the table to go quiet Frisky, I heard Mom ask Carol, "What about the bows on the almonds? Peach or white?"

I didn't wait to hear Carol's answer. I wasn't sure if I'd ever want to see another almond again after the wedding. But at least I had permission to keep Pigsy Wigsy for the week. I couldn't wait. I just knew that P.W. was going to be the best pet yet.

Three

"I'M going now," I announced to Mom and Carol in the kitchen the next morning. They were stuffing mushrooms with some kind of bread crumb and cheese mixture. Carol wore an apron, and her hair was tied up in a scarf. She didn't look anything like a person about to get married. She just looked like the same old Carol.

"Where are you going?" Mom asked.

"Over to Mrs . Pinkston's to pick up P.W."

"All right, but make sure you're home by 11 o'clock, because the seamstress will be here for your gown fitting."

"No problem, Mom," I said. "Lynn is coming with me to help carry P.W.'s food and stuff. I'll only have to make one trip."

Lynn's front door slammed at the same time as mine, and we met each other on the lawn between our houses.

"Ready?" Lynn asked. "What did your parents say?"

I shrugged. "They said fine. It's okay to keep P.W. for the week."

"Wow!" said Lynn. "I want to move in with you. Fish just aren't very much fun. You can't walk them or play with them. They don't even bark."

"They're pretty to look at," I said, trying to cheer her up.

"Face it, Sherri. They're boring."

"Well, you can help me with Pigsy Wigsy."

"Thanks."

On the way to Mrs. Pinkston's house we stopped by the Rolstons to put out the cat food. I planned to check up on the hermit crabs in the afternoon. It was neat living in a rural area because people own all different types of pets.

Mrs. Pinkston lived two streets from us in a big Spanish-style house with a large fenced yard. A woman met us at the door before we even rang the bell.

"Thank goodness you're here!" she told us. She pushed her glasses up higher on her nose and snapped a dishrag in the air. "I simply *can't* clean this house properly with a pig running around loose!"

"Who are you and where's Mrs. Pinkston?" I asked. I knew it sounded rude, but the way she had snapped the dishrag surprised the politeness right out of me.

"I'm Mrs. Reed, Mrs. Pinkston's part-time housekeeper," the woman answered. "Mrs. Pinkston left on an early flight this morning, and I'm here to do a thorough spring cleaning while she's gone. Which one of you is Sherri?"

"Me," I said.

Mrs. Reed handed me a list. "These are the instructions Mrs. Pinkston left for the animal's care," she said. She pointed to a pile of bags and rags near the door. "Those are his blankets and food." Mrs. Reed wrinkled her nose. "I can't wait to get that offending snippet of pig flesh out of this house!"

"Thanks," I said, trying not to smile at the funny way Mrs. Reed talked. "Where is he?"

"Just a minute. I locked him in the bathroom. I didn't think he could hurt much in there."

As soon as Mrs. Reed left to go get Pigsy Wigsy, Lynn and I started giggling.

"She sure doesn't like pigs, does she?" Lynn whispered.

"How could you tell?" I whispered back. Then I tried to put on a serious expression like Mrs. Reed's. "Where *is* that offending snippet of pig flesh, anyway?" I mimicked. "Do you think he escaped from the bathroom and is running wild on the carpets?"

Lynn put both hands on her cheeks and made her mouth into a surprised "O." "I certainly hope not," she said, pretending to be in a panic. "What if he oinks in the living room or something?"

"Or grunts in the kitchen?" I said through my giggles.

"Or snorts in the bedroom?" Lynn did an imitation of a pig snort, and we burst out laughing.

"Help! Help!" I cried in a high, squeaky voice. "That snippet of pig flesh snorted at me!"

The thought of a pig chasing Mrs. Reed around the house oinking, grunting, and snorting just about did us in. We both made pig noises and laughed until tears ran down our faces.

I was about to grunt again when Mrs. Reed came back. We quickly wiped our eyes and swallowed our giggles. Mrs. Reed had Pigsy Wigsy on a leash and she was holding him as far away from her as possible.

"He's all yours," she said. She handed the leash to me with the tips of two fingers. "It

smells better in here already!"

I curled the leash around my wrist and took a good look at Pigsy Wigsy. He was mostly black, but he had a little patch of white on his head. His back sort of dipped, and his belly hung low to the ground. His legs looked like tree stumps, and his head was so big I wondered if he ever got tired from holding it up. If I squinted until my vision got blurry, I could almost imagine he was a bulldog.

"The sooner that... *beast* is out of here, the better!" said Mrs. Reed.

Poor P.W. He looked up at me with soft, brown eyes, then pushed his snout gently against my leg. I thought I could almost imagine how he felt. I had to defend him.

"Pigs are actually very clean animals, Mrs. Reed," I said. "They don't roll around in mud unless people let them." I had heard that somewhere, maybe at school. "Pigs are also smart. These Vietnamese potbellied pigs can actually be trained to use a litter box like cats do."

"Be that as it may," Mrs. Reed said, scowling at P.W., "it will be a lot easier to straighten up without a pig around."

"I guess so," I said, reaching down to pet P.W. I had seen potbellied pigs before, but I had never touched one. P.W. didn't feel much like a dog, but his bristly coat was smooth. I began to realize how different this job was going to be.

P.W. snorted, and I grinned. "We're going to get along just fine!" I told him.

Lynn picked up the bags and blankets, and we started to leave.

"Oh, one more thing," Mrs. Reed said. "Make sure to walk that pig by the park so that it can heed the call of nature. I haven't had time. In fact, I hope there isn't a present for me in the bathroom." She shuddered.

"No problem," I said, happy to get away. "Poor Pigsy Wigsy," I crooned as soon as we reached the sidewalk. I heard Mrs. Pinkston's door slam shut behind us. "You're such a sweet

little thing. How can that lady be so nasty toward you?"

Lynn and I reached down to pat P.W. at the same time. Pigsy looked at us, then snorted playfully and pulled on his leash. He tugged in the direction of the park.

"He sure seems glad to be away from that awful Mrs. Reed," said Lynn. "Look how frisky he is!"

"I think *anyone* would be glad to be away from that woman," I said. "And if you think he's happy now, just wait until you see how happy he gets when he's at my house where people actually *like* pets. I think Mom and Dad will be tickled pink with this pig."

Four

"ISN'T P.W. just about the cutest thing you ever saw?" I said as Lynn and I strolled through the park a few minutes later. "I'm so glad I'm taking care of him!"

"He reminds me of Wilbur in *Charlotte's Web*," Lynn said.

"But Wilbur was huge," I said, thinking back to the pig in E.B. White's novel.

"Yes, but he was cute. Of course, P.W. is small enough to pick up," she added.

"Yeah, isn't that cool!" I said. "It's like having a baby pig forever. And even though Mrs. Pinkston has only had P.W. for a little while, she told me that he surprised her several times

43

with how smart he is." I watched P.W. sniff at a leaf on the ground. His ears pricked up and he looked at me.

"He knows we're talking about him," Lynn said excitedly. She bent down. "Here, Pigsy Wigsy!" she called, slapping her hands on her legs. P.W. trotted over to her and obligingly sniffed her hand. "You're so fat and cute," she told him as she petted his back. "Not exactly soft," she added with a laugh. "But cute."

"He *is* fat!" I agreed. "Look at the way his stomach sticks out on both sides and the way he waddles. He looks like a miniature blimp."

"I doubt he'll float away, though," Lynn said with a giggle.

"Nope. I think Pigsy definitely has four feet planted firmly on the ground."

"I wonder how he'll get along with Frisky," Lynn said.

"We'll have to wait and see, I guess," I said. "They'll probably do fine. I've been reading up on pigs since Mrs. Pinkston offered me this job, and the books say they get along well with other household pets."

"I'm impressed," Lynn said. "Do you always look stuff up on pets before you sit for them?"

"Only if it's an animal I don't already know about," I answered. "Before I started my pet-sitting business I knew how to take care of dogs, cats, fish, and birds, but not snakes or horses. And," I added, looking down at P.W., "not pigs!"

"After this week you'll be an expert."

We wandered around the park, showing off P.W. to all the people passing by who wanted to stop and talk about our unusual pet.

"Your pet-sitting business has become quite exotic," Mrs. Kink said as she jogged past us. "First pythons and now pigs."

"The more unusual, the better I like it," I replied.

"We'd better not introduce my snake to that pig, though," Mrs. Kink called back over her shoulder.

"I know," I said. "He might think P.W. is a tasty morsel."

"Yuck," Lynn said.

"Are you taking care of livestock now?" Mr. Hemple asked as he rode by on his horse, Miwok. I had fed and exercised Miwok one weekend when Mr. Hemple went away.

"Only horses and pigs so far."

"I know someone with a cow you could watch," Mr. Hemple said jokingly.

"I don't think my parents would let me bring a cow home. Besides, I'm not allowed to go out of the neighborhood," I replied as he rode off.

"How about a calf?" Lynn asked.

"*That* would be fun," I said. "Maybe I'll ask my parents now, just in case it ever comes up."

By the time I arrived home it was half past eleven. The living room looked as if it had been struck by a hurricane. Carol was standing on a stool in the middle of the floor. The seamstress was working around her. The seamstress's assistant was jotting down numbers.

Bolts of material were leaning against the coffee table and one wall. What seemed like yards of lace were draped across chairs. A big sewing basket was opened in the middle of the floor.

"I'm going to be the ugliest bride in the history of the world!" Carol wailed at the top of her lungs. "This dress makes me look like a tank in lace. I'm supposed to look tall and thin and willowy, not short and lumpy and dumpy! Mother, help!"

"Sherri, you're late!" Mom shouted the minute I showed up in the doorway with P.W. standing shyly behind me.

"I'm sorry. We walked through the park so that P.W. could... you know."

"That's no excuse! I told you 11 o'clock!"

Why was everyone so upset? What did it matter if I was a little late? Carol was still being fitted, and there wasn't room for two of us on the stool. But, I reminded myself, mothers are like that—especially when a panic is going on. And a panic was definitely going on.

"Mother!" Carol shouted again. "Will you look at this? The collar is too high and my hair hangs over!"

"You can wear your hair up, Carol," Mom said.

"Then my veil won't fit right."

"Why don't you cut your hair?" I suggested, trying to keep P.W. behind me. He was tugging on his leash, probably trying to escape the craziness.

Carol glared at me from the top of the stool. "Cut my hair!" she practically screamed. "That's just the type of stupid comment I'd expect from someone who brings a pig into the house."

"A PIG!" the seamstress and her assistant shouted at the same time.

"A PIG!" my mother echoed. "Where's a pig?" She ran over to me and took a good look.

By now, Pigsy Wigsy was having a little panic of his own. As the noise and shouting increased, he became more nervous. He backed out into the hall. He pulled on his leash so hard that I stumbled backward.

"Sherri, who gave you permission to bring a pig into this house?" Mom shouted. "Of all the silly, ridiculous things to do!"

I started to remind her that *she* had given me permission last night at the dinner table, but the words never made it out of my mouth. The seamstress went after Pigsy Wigsy with a yardstick. Pigsy, terrified, snapped the leash out of my hand and took off.

"Eeee! Eeee!" Squealing and snorting, P.W. stampeded through the piles of lace and material. The seamstress's assistant lunged for him, but missed and ended up elbow-first in the sewing basket.

Patterns and material flew in every direction as Pigsy plowed through the living room. He tromped on a bowl full of seed pearls, sending them flying. They scattered like rain, plinking on the wood floor. The seamstress charged after the pig, slipped on the pearls, and landed on her bottom with a thump.

"Eeee! Eeee!" Pigsy squealed as his hooves landed on the pearls and he skidded into the wall. But he was up and running a split second later, heading straight for Carol's stool.

Carol lifted her dress and screamed for help. My mother charged to the other side of the room and blocked the door. Pigsy spun around just in time and headed back in my direction. He was trailing lace and ribbons behind him.

No one could catch him. Mom was running in one direction. The seamstress and her assistant were running in the other direction. The dining room looked like a snow storm of material and lace. Carol was stomping her feet and squealing almost as much as the pig. I would have laughed if the grown-ups hadn't been so serious.

"Do something, Sherri!" Carol yelled. "Do something before my whole wedding is ruined!"

Finally, Pigsy raced by me. "I've got him!" I shouted. I grabbed a sheet hanging over the back of the nearest chair and threw it over him. But potbellied pigs are faster and stronger than they look. Pigsy pulled me along with him for at least 10 feet before we both slid to a halt right in front of my mother. I pulled Pigsy Wigsy half onto my lap, unwrapped the sheet, and soothed him.

I didn't want to look up. Instead, I stared at my mother's tapping foot. "Do you know what you just did?" she asked, her voice barely controlled.

"I caught the pig?" I whispered. Somehow I don't think that was the answer that she wanted.

"You *ruined* the tablecloth for the buffet!"

I looked down at the cover I had thrown over Pigsy to catch him. "Oh. It looked like a sheet. I didn't know."

"Obviously!" Mom said.

"It's not ruined," I protested. "It isn't even dirty!"

Carol yanked a hand through her hair and

shouted, "But it was touched by a pig! A dirty, stinking pig! Who wants to eat off of it after *that*? I can't believe you would do this to me!"

"Do what?" I shouted back. "You're the ones who scared him. And he is not dirty. Pigs are cleaner than people!"

"I will repeat my earlier question," Mother said calmly—too calmly. "Who gave you permission to bring that pig into this house?"

"*You* did, Mom! Last night at the dinner table. I told you that I was going to take care of Mrs. Pinkston's pig for a week while she's on her business trip to England. You said okay. You *did!*"

"Well, Mrs. Pinkston can just make other arrangements," Mom said, "because we are not—and I repeat—not going to have a pig in this house. How could you even think of bringing it here when we're getting ready for the wedding? I want that pig out of the house right now!"

"But I can't!" I told her, hugging P.W. to me.

"Of course you can," Carol told me. "Just take him back to Mrs. Pinkston and tell her to put him in a kennel for the week."

"But Mrs. Pinkston is already gone," I said, my eyes filling with tears. "I *have* to take care of Pigsy Wigsy. I promised. And I told you last night. I really did."

Mother folded her arms across her chest. All was silent while she stared at me. Then her finger came up and she slowly pointed straight at P.W. "Okay, the pig stays," she said.

"Mother!" Carol wailed.

"The pig stays," Mother continued. "Apparently, it's as much my fault that he's here as it is yours, Sherri. I clearly wasn't paying attention at the table last night." She kept pointing at P.W., but she was staring at me. "But understand that I don't want to *see* him, or *hear* him, or *SMELL* him even once!"

"Okay," I promised quickly. "You won't even know we're here."

"I'd better not, or *else!*"

"Or else?" I said with a gulp.

"Or else I'll be tempted to turn him into an hors d'oeuvre!"

Mom didn't have to tell me twice. I grabbed P.W., took a good grip on the leash, and headed to my room. I promised myself that Pigsy would be the most invisible pig on the face of the earth *and* in the history of the world. I wasn't going to push my luck.

Five

"I don't know what their problem is, P.W.,"
I told the pig a few minutes later. Pigsy
was examining my room while I fixed up a bed
for him in the corner. He looked up at me and
grunted. Then he trotted over. "They're so busy
that they don't even have time to listen," I said.
"If they would just get to know you they would
find out that you're wonderful."

I ruffled the bristles on the back of P.W.'s
neck. He tipped his snout up to snuffle my
hand. "See," I said, "you're friendly and affec-
tionate. And you're not dirty at all. I would eat
off that dumb old tablecloth!"

P.W. seemed to understand the word "eat."

The minute I said it, he nuzzled my hand and looked at me as if he were waiting for something. I poured half a cup of pig chow in his dish, just like Mrs. Pinkston's instructions said. P.W. had his nose in it before I set it down. In seconds, he seemed glued to the dish.

"You must be starved," I said, chuckling. "I'll bet Mrs. Reed didn't feed you at all."

I watched P.W. eat for a moment. Then I poked around in the food bag Mrs. Pinkston had sent. It contained grapes, apples, raisins, and an assortment of vegetables. P.W. looked up when he heard the bag rustle and trotted over to investigate. He shoved his head against the bag and looked at me with hopeful eyes.

"No way, you big hog!" I said, laughing. "I'm putting this up until later, and then it's going in the refrigerator out of your reach."

"Sherri!" Mother called as I was putting the bag up on my top shelf. "Come get fitted for your dress."

"Coming," I called back. I turned to P.W.

"Now, listen. We don't want to get into trouble, so you had better stay put. I'm going to shut the door. If you're tired, go to sleep." I pointed to his bed. "I'll be back as fast as I can."

But the dress fitting seemed to take forever. I was supposed to stand without moving. By the time the seamstress and her assistant had finished pinning up the hem, my legs felt as if they were stuck in concrete. And there was more to be done!

"If you would stop fidgeting, it would be a lot easier," Mom said.

"I can't help it. I'm tired."

"We're all tired," Carol said. "There are a million more things to do, and time is running out."

"I'll help," I offered, but they weren't listening. They were discussing whether to have candles on the indoor buffet tables. Mom thought candles and flowers were elegant together. Carol thought wax might drip into the food.

I wiggled some more, and the seamstress

mumbled something. I couldn't make out what she said, because she had a ton of pins clenched between her lips. I hated standing there in that itchy dress. What I really wanted to do was check on Pigsy. After all, I hadn't had time to pig-proof my room and Pigsy *was* a pig. What if he was rooting around in my stuff? I wondered if I had given him enough time out-side.

Finally, I was allowed to take off the lacy peach and white dress and escape to my room. I half expected to find my clothes dragged all over the floor. Instead, I found P.W. sleeping in the bed I had made for him. He was snoring softly. I would have shouted for my mother and sister to come see what an adorable pig he was, but I didn't want to wake him. He must have been completely tuckered out from all that run-ning and chasing earlier.

I decided to call Lynn.

"I was just thinking about you and Pigsy Wigsy," she said when she answered the phone.

"How's it going?"

"Not well. Horrible, in fact. We've been banished to my room."

"Why?" Lynn asked.

"Because Carol hates pigs," I said. "She totally freaked out when I brought P.W. home. You should have heard her. She stood on the stool in the living room and squealed."

Lynn laughed.

"It's not funny," I said gloomily. "Mom doesn't remember giving me permission to have P.W. here for the week. She said she doesn't want to see, hear, or smell him, or she'll turn him into an hors d'oeuvre."

"What a drag!" Lynn said. "I wish I could take him off your hands, but you know my mom would flip out worse than yours."

"I know," I said. "Thanks for offering. And actually, you could help me out in another way."

"How?"

"Could you walk Rusty for me this afternoon and check up on the Hoopers' hermit crabs? I can get to the Rolstons' cats, but I think I'd better stick around here as much as possible—at least until everybody cools off."

"Sure thing," Lynn said.

We were quiet for a minute, thinking our private thoughts. Then Lynn asked, "What's Pigsy doing now?"

"Sleeping. After Mom, Carol, and the dressmakers chased him around the living room, he was exhausted."

"They actually chased him?"

Even though I was in trouble, I found myself grinning then. "Yeah. It was like something out of a slapstick comedy," I said. "I finally caught him after he had dragged half of the lace and material all around the room. It's pretty funny when you think about it."

Lynn giggled. "I take it your mom didn't see the humor in the situation."

"Why do you think I'm in my room?" I said.

P.W. was still sleeping soundly when my

mother called me a couple of hours later. After talking to Lynn, I had dashed out to feed the Rolstons' cats. But other than that I had spent the entire afternoon in my room reading. Pigsy had slept through everything. Of course, he wouldn't sleep forever, so I left my door open just a crack. I figured I would hear him if he woke up and started squealing.

When I arrived in the kitchen, Mom handed me a stack of plates. "I need you to set the table, Sherri."

"Okay." I looked around. The house was quiet for the first time all afternoon. "Where's Carol?"

"She went to the delicatessen to make sure her order for cheese is in. She wants to start making the food trays tomorrow and freeze what she can so that she has less work on Friday."

"Carol should have just had someone else do the food for the reception," I said as I placed the plates around the table. "She seems a little stressed out."

Mom handed me a clean dish towel and pointed to the glasses in the dish drainer. "Carol is trying to save money *and* she wants everything to be perfect."

"Yes, but she's just not acting like herself lately," I said as I dried the glasses. Carol was usually very levelheaded and organized. I had watched her put together the food for other people's weddings, and she was always the calm person.

"Having that pig in the house hasn't helped matters," Mom said sternly.

"I'm sorry you're all so upset about P.W.," I told her. "But you said—"

"I know. I know. Just keep him out of our way until after the wedding," Mom said.

"I hope that Carol returns to normal after the wedding," I remarked as I dried the last glass.

"I'm sure she will. There is just so much to do and not enough hands to do it with."

"I wish John were here," I said.

"So do I!" Carol said, suddenly storming into the kitchen. "It's impossible to do everything myself." She threw her purse on the counter and plopped down into the nearest chair.

Instantly the calm atmosphere in the kitchen became super-charged.

"What happened at the deli?" Mom asked, turning to Carol.

"You won't believe this," Carol said. "They haven't even *ordered* the cheeses yet! The wedding is less than a week away, and I can't even put together my trays. What am I going to do?"

"We'll just have to do other things and put together the food at the last minute," Mother said.

Carol slumped. "There are only so many last minutes."

"I'll help," I said. "I'll tie almonds into the nets and count jelly beans into the swans. I can arrange flowers and tie bows. Just tell me what to do."

"Finish setting the table," Mom said.

Carol just shook her head. "I wish there were four of me," she muttered.

I shook my head, too. Ten years old was old enough to do more than set the dumb table. I was going to have to find something to do and surprise them.

Six

I couldn't stand being in the same room with Carol when she was spouting off, so I headed for the yard to visit Frisky. No one even noticed I was leaving. I sighed and picked up Frisky's favorite stick.

"Hey, Frisky!" I called out. "Want to fetch?" I threw the stick and watched Frisky bound after it. "Good puppy," I said when he brought it back. "At least *you* still love me."

Frisky barked and leaped in the air, trying to get the stick.

"Go!" I shouted as I heaved it across the yard. "I wish I could bring P.W. out to meet you. Maybe tomorrow."

We played for about 15 minutes before Dad came home. I followed him into the house and washed my hands. Dad and Mom told each other about their days. Then a little while later Dad carried a piping hot dish of eggplant Parmesan to the table. I brought the salad and the dressing, and Mom brought steamed carrots and a covered basket of bread.

"And then there's a problem with the music," Carol complained the minute everyone was served. I took a bite of my eggplant, and thought about what I could do to help Carol so she would turn back into the sister I knew and loved.

I was about halfway through with my salad when I felt something wet nudge my knee. I reached down to scratch and my hand touched pig. My eyes opened wide. I started to choke on a carrot. In seconds I was coughing so hard that tears began to block my vision.

Everyone shut up for a minute. Dad reached over and thumped me on the back until I stopped coughing.

"Are you all right, Sherri?" Mom asked, concern all over her face. Even Carol looked worried for a minute.

But I nodded and forced myself to smile until everyone seemed satisfied. Dad told me not to eat so fast. Carol said I should take a sip of water. Then they all turned their attention back to Carol's problem with the wedding music.

I was in a panic. I had to get Pigsy out of there. But how was I going to smuggle a pig past my parents and sister? I reached under the table and petted Pigsy's snout. I tried to send him a mental message: *Good Pigsy*, I thought as loudly as I could. *Just stay with Sherri and everything will be all right.*

Suddenly he was gone. I tapped my foot around under the table, but I couldn't feel him anywhere. I bit my lip and worried about where he would turn up next.

I didn't have to wait long. First my sister

and then my mom reached down to scratch the tickle from Pigsy's hairy sniffs. Dad slapped his leg as though he had been bitten by a bug. I was sure I could hear Pigsy shuffling out of the way.

I closed my eyes and thought fast. I couldn't let them investigate further. Pigsy would be out on his ear, and I would be out of a job.

Then I had a great idea. I wiped the dressing off a piece of lettuce from my salad and hung it under the table. I waved it around a little and hoped that Pigsy would notice. He did. I felt him snatch the lettuce from my fingers.

Without being obvious, I passed him a carrot next. If I could just keep him busy until everyone had finished eating, then offer to clear the table, he—and I—would be safe.

"It just seems like everything that can go wrong is going wrong," Carol complained. "I mean, I planned and made lists and thought I had everything under control, but nothing is

working out the way it's supposed to."

That's the understatement of the year! I thought. I crossed my fingers and hoped that they were almost done.

Unfortunately, Carol was taking about a hundred years to eat her salad. She hadn't even started on the eggplant yet. I watched her stab a piece of lettuce with her fork. She brought the lettuce toward her mouth, but stopped suddenly to talk some more instead.

"I just don't understand how everything has gotten so out of hand," Carol said. She waved her fork like a wand. A shiny drop of dressing flew off the lettuce. No one noticed but me. Carol sighed. "I guess I just can't rely on anyone but myself," she said. Jab, jab, went her fork.

Then Mom started doing it, too! "You have to calm down and take things one step at a time," she said, her fork pointed toward Carol. A radish wobbled from its tip.

"I *am* calm," Carol declared with another

poke from her lettuce.

"Not calm enough," Mom said. She shook her fork and her head at the same time.

I watched the radish punch the air with every word. I couldn't believe it wasn't falling off.

"You're going to wear yourself out," Mom went on. "And then what? What good will all of your preparations do if you're too tired to enjoy the wedding?" She brought the fork to her mouth, then paused. "You really need to think about that, Carol."

Oh, brother! I wanted to scream. *Just eat!*

Underneath the table I handed Pigsy a hunk of cucumber. How much longer could my luck hold out?

"You're probably right," said Carol. "At least we're sitting down to a nice family dinner," she said. "I haven't had a chance to sit down and relax all day." She ate her lettuce and leaned back in her chair.

Finally, I thought.

Then disaster struck. In the silence that followed Carol's last statement, Pigsy burped.

I put my hand over my mouth, but there was no disguising it. It was a huge, gigantic hog burp, and it seemed to go on for at least 10 seconds.

"SHERRI!" Carol screamed, yanking the tablecloth up and staring at Pigsy. "How *could* you?"

"I didn't do it on purpose," I began. "Pigsy is just trying to be friendly."

As if to prove my point, Pigsy shuffled over to Carol and licked her knee. "He licked me!" Carol shrieked. "Oh, gross! I'm going to die of pig poisoning!"

"You can't die of pig poisoning," I said.

"With my luck," said Carol, "I'd be the first! They'll have to write me up in the paper—'Bride Dies of Pig Contamination on Eve of Her Wedding'!"

For a second, I almost smiled. I thought Carol was making a joke. She wasn't. She jumped to her feet and threw her napkin on the table. "I can't take this anymore! First the food, then the music and now... this!" She pushed her plate away. "That pig has killed my appetite!" she said hotly.

"It's not like P.W. even touched your food," I put in quickly. "You can still eat it."

"I'm too disgusted to eat!" Carol said. "I'm going to go call John. Wait until he hears about this!"

Carol ran off toward the living room to tattle on me to John. I slowly turned back to face my parents.

Mom simply pointed toward my room, her face a stone mask.

"I'm going. I'm going," I said while I hauled Pigsy out from under the table. We headed down the hall. I heard Carol's hysterical voice on the phone with John as I passed the living room. Pigsy snorted a loud one, and I was glad.

"Whoever heard of a person dying of pig poisoning?" I asked Pigsy a moment later when we were safely inside my room. "A burp and a lick are no big deal."

I slumped in my chair and tried not to cry. P.W. struggled into my lap, hooves and all. He nuzzled my hand and looked at me with adoring eyes. At least someone understood me, even if that someone was a pig. Either that or he was hungry. I put him down and got his food sack from the shelf. Right now, I was glad I had forgotten to put his food in the refrigerator. Seeing Carol and Mom right now was the last thing I wanted to do.

After rummaging for a second, I dug an apple from P.W.'s sack and held it out for him. Pigsy didn't waste a second chowing it down.

"Why is everything always my fault lately?" I asked Pigsy. "And Carol—she's such a wimp! Why is she their favorite? Moving away really changed her. She used to be fun to be around. We used to sit on her bed and have long talks. Now all she does is fuss about her wedding."

After awhile I got tired of talking to P.W. and

started reading a book. While P.W. rooted imaginary vegetables in my rug, I played three games of solitaire. While P.W. opened my cupboards with his snout and investigated, I waited for someone to come get me. Whenever my parents sent me to my room, they would come by a little later to have a talk. I guessed they were so mad this time that I would be stuck in my room forever.

Two hours later, *I* started getting mad. I peeked out of my door and heard voices in the living room. Mom and Dad and Carol were talking about the wedding as if they had forgotten all about me. I went back to my bed and sat down, thinking hard.

"P.W.," I said at last, "I don't understand it. You're not a nuisance and I'm sure Carol would see that if she just got to know you better." P.W. grunted and pushed his snout into my leg. "It's too bad she's never going to get the chance."

Seven

"I 'VE spent more time in my room over the past three days than I have since Carol moved away," I told Lynn on Monday. Mom had finally allowed her to come over. "It seems like every time anyone even *sees* P.W., I get sent to my room."

"That doesn't seem fair," Lynn said as she scratched Pigsy Wigsy behind the ears. "Anyone can see that P.W. is a good pig."

"Not according to Carol," I said. "According to Carol, Pigsy is the worst pig in the history of the world."

"What happened besides the lace race?"

"Only a couple of things."

"Like…?"

"You'll never believe this," I said. "Saturday after dinner, Carol was in her room fixing her hair, and Pigsy sneaked in. He climbed up on some boxes that she had stacked by the bed and got on the bed."

"Did she see him in the mirror?" Lynn asked.

"It might have been better for Pigsy if she had. Instead, she sat on him."

"Sat?" Lynn repeated, her eyes opening wide.

"I don't know who squealed the loudest— Carol or P.W. When I ran to her room I found P.W. hiding behind the bed and Carol sitting in the pile of boxes. It was pretty funny until she accused me of letting him in her room on purpose—and Mom agreed with her."

"I wish I had been there," Lynn said, laughing.

"That wasn't the best part, though," I said. I started laughing too. "On Sunday, Carol was really freaked out because the flowers were going to be late or something. Anyway, she was sitting like a zombie in the middle of the family room floor, eating ice cream out of the carton and moaning."

"Yeah?" Lynn prompted, still smiling.

"Well, the phone rang, and while she was talking to someone from the band, Pigsy somehow escaped from my room again. He snorted up half of her ice cream while she was on the phone. I was watching TV and didn't notice him until it was too late."

"Wow! Carol must have really been mad when she saw him," said Lynn.

I giggled. "She didn't see him right away. She came back in and started eating her ice cream."

"Oooh! And you didn't say anything?" asked Lynn.

I shrugged. "I thought about it, but Pigsy had wandered away and well... everything just happened too quickly! And then, when Carol

dived right back into her ice cream, I thought I'd better *not* say anything at all. Unfortunately, just when I started to relax, Pigsy strolled out from behind the chair with ice cream all over his snout! Carol started chasing him around the family room and screaming about pig poisoning. Naturally, I got sent to my room again."

"Naturally."

"But it wasn't my fault. I can't help it if the latch on my door doesn't hold." I looked at Lynn and she looked at me, and we both burst out laughing again.

P.W. was busy sniffing the stuffed animals that I keep lined up on the floor by my bed. As we watched, he tipped over Choco Crocodile. He pushed it across the floor with his snout until it bumped into the wall. P.W. looked at me and snorted.

"Good job, P.W.," I said. "You're quite the little bulldozer."

That small bit of praise sent him trotting back over to the animals.

"Look," Lynn said. "He's going to do it again."

I giggled as P.W. nosed Ted D. Bear, Margaret Monkey, and Ducky Lucky from the pile to the wall.

"I guess moving things is his favorite hobby," I said to Lynn. "He was having a great time pushing the pillows in the living room yesterday until Mom threw a fit. I don't know why. He wasn't hurting anything."

"Poor, misunderstood P.W.," Lynn crooned. "What did you get? The room?"

"The room," I confirmed, shaking my head. "No wonder P.W. wants to redecorate. He's probably just as tired of it as I am."

When he started nudging open my closet door I said, "Come on. Let's take Pigsy for a walk around the house."

Lynn looked at me with wide eyes. "You mean on *purpose?* I thought your parents and sister didn't want to see Pigsy. I thought you just said that you'd be sent to your room."

I grinned mischievously. "I've had it! I'm tired of being treated like a baby. I've tried being good, but it doesn't make any difference. If Carol is feeling crazy, then it's her own fault. Besides, I'll make sure he's on his leash."

I got the leash on P.W., opened the door to my room and led Pigsy into the hall. "If they *think* I'm so horrible, I might as well *be* horrible," I told Lynn. "I get punished just the same."

Lynn and I strolled around the house with P.W. in plain sight of everyone. Carol scowled from the top of the ladder in the family room. She was hanging silk flower baskets. Mom shook her head and pointed outdoors as we passed her in the kitchen. Dad sort of smiled and rolled his eyes as we went by his study. Secretly, I think Dad saw the humor in the whole situation. He just didn't want to take sides.

"That wasn't so bad," Lynn commented as we went outside.

"Let's play with P.W. in front of the family

room window," I suggested, glancing in to make sure that Carol could see us. Carol frowned again. She could see us just fine.

"You're terrible!" Lynn told me.

"I know," I said, grinning.

Just then, Frisky barked from the side of the yard.

"Why don't we introduce Frisky to P.W.," I suggested.

"Cool!" Lynn replied.

Frisky went wild the minute he saw Pigsy. He raced over and stuck his nose right in P.W.'s face. Frisky's tail wagged a mile a minute while P.W. just stood there. He didn't even twitch.

Frisky backed up and barked: "Arf, arf."

P.W. grunted: "Unk, unk."

Lynn and I just laughed and watched as the two of them suddenly sprang into action. First P.W. took the lead, and Frisky chased him in a circle around the backyard. Then Frisky passed him on the turn, and P.W. frolicked along behind.

"Look at them go!" Lynn cried.

"We should call P.W. 'Fearless,'" I said. "I think he thinks he's a dog, too."

A few minutes later both pets were tired. Frisky loped toward us and put his paws on my leg. P.W. trotted toward us and put his hooves on my leg.

"Ouch!" I yelped. "I suppose you guys are hungry?"

"Arf!"

"Unk!"

"Okay, okay. Lynn, can you watch them while I go get a snack?"

"Sure."

While Lynn tossed a leaf in the air to entertain Frisky and P.W., I went into the kitchen for dog biscuits and grapes. Just as I opened the refrigerator, I heard the clatter of little hooves on the linoleum. A second later P.W. stuck his head into the refrigerator and poked his snout greedily into the bag of grapes. He was also only an inch away from the the first batch of hors d'oeuvres.

"Oh, Pigsy! You're such a greedy little pig," I teased. "Come on. Let's go back out to the yard before someone sees you."

P.W. followed me back out to the yard, as loyal as any puppy.

After I gave Frisky and P.W. their treats, we played for awhile longer, and then Lynn had to go home. "I know it's not possible, but every time I see P.W., he looks fatter," she said as she was leaving.

"Lynn," I said, "he *is* a pig." I checked out P.W.'s bulging sides and shrugged. "He's just healthy, I guess."

"But maybe he should at least get more exercise," Lynn suggested. "Even for a pig, he seems fat. He might be putting on weight because he's stuck in your room doing nothing for so long."

"Okay. I'll run him around the yard some more before I go in."

P.W. and I chased each other around the

yard until we were both tired. I noticed that Carol had left the family room.

"Come on, P.W.," I said. "Let's go find a project."

We went into the house and found Carol at the kitchen counter. She was rolling zucchini balls in cracker crumbs. On the table behind her was the first tray she had prepared. Pigsy sniffed the air hungrily.

"May I help?" I asked, keeping a tight hold on Pigsy's leash.

"No," Carol said.

"Why not?" I asked. "I've made zucchini balls before. I'm good at it."

Carol turned to me, looked down at Pigsy with disgust, then looked back up at me. "No, you can't help. You've been playing with that *swine* all morning. Any hand that touched swine will never touch my zucchini balls!" she declared.

"I could wash my hands," I said.

"It wouldn't do any good," Carol said. "Why

91

don't you just trot off and play with your pig."

In other words, I thought, *"Get lost!"*

I stomped off with Pigsy in tow. I knew it was babyish and that she wouldn't even see, but as I passed behind Carol, I touched one of her precious zucchini balls with a finger.

So there! I thought.

Eight

F OR the next two days it seemed like "get lost" was all I heard. On Tuesday I tried to help iron the tablecloths, but Carol said I was too slow and sloppy. She did it herself, and then complained about how much time it wasted. It was a good thing I had P.W., Frisky, Cookoo, and all my pet-sitting jobs to keep me busy.

On Wednesday morning I got up early and made French toast for the whole family. I'm pretty good at French toast. P.W. followed me around the kitchen. He nudged the refrigerator every time he caught me looking his way.

"If I didn't know better, I'd think you were

93

starving to death," I told him. I fed him some grapes and a salad that I made out of raw potatoes, carrots, and apples. "You're like a living garbage disposal!"

All P.W. said was, "Unk!" He was too busy eating.

"You're a spoiled beggar, but I love you," I told him.

"Unk!"

I was sure that meant he loved me too, in pig talk. I hooked his leash to his collar, then fastened it to the door leading from the kitchen to the garage. He sprawled on the floor, and I gave him a pat on the head. Nothing awful had happened in the last two days. Mom hadn't said anything, but I noticed she was putting up with the sight of P.W.—as long as he was on his leash and well out of the way.

"Come on everybody!" I called. "Breakfast is ready." I was really proud of myself. I had made orange juice and set the table. I had even folded the napkins in triangles and put them

under the forks on the left side of each plate. I thought I had finally done something that my parents and sister would appreciate.

Dad was the first person in the kitchen. "Mmm, I'm starved," he said. "It looks delicious, Sherri." He sat down and poured syrup on his French toast.

Mom came in, stood next to the table, and drank her glass of orange juice.

"Have some toast, Mom," I offered.

"No, thanks—I have to run," she said. "In the middle of all this, I can't believe I promised Jared's that I would do the windows for the store's spring sale. Bye!"

"But, Mom," I said, "what about breakfast?"

When she didn't answer or come back, my shoulders slumped. Then I straightened up again as Carol came in. Maybe my effort wasn't all lost.

"French toast?" I asked, pointing toward her spot at the table.

"No way!" Carol said. "I'm too stressed out

to eat. Besides," she said, glancing at P.W., "I wouldn't eat in the same room as a pig if you paid me!"

I couldn't stand it. I had to say something. "You wouldn't want to eat it, anyway. P.W. likes French toast almost as much as he likes ice cream. I let him lick yours before I put it on your plate!"

"You're sickening!" Carol cried.

"And he burped in your milk. In fact," I went on, "I let him break the eggs beneath his hooves and stir the batter with his tail. So there!"

"Grow up," Carol retorted. "You're just trying to make me mad."

"I don't have to try very hard," I snapped.

"That's enough, girls," Dad broke in. "If you don't have something nice to say—"

"She started it," I said.

Carol pressed her lips together and made a sound like she wanted to say something mean and nasty. Instead, she walked out of the kitchen in a huff.

97

I sat down across from Dad and ate my meal in silence. Even the fact that he gobbled up all the rest of the French toast didn't improve my mood.

"Don't let her get to you," Dad said. "Just mind your own business and leave Carol alone."

I cleaned up the kitchen—not that anyone cared—and wandered toward my room with P.W. On my way I stopped in front of the door to the spare bedroom. It was slightly open and I could see buckets of flowers on the floor. They had just been delivered. Mom and Carol were going to make corsages and centerpieces for the tables.

Here's something I can do, I thought. "Come on, P.W., we can snip the stem ends off of the carnations as well as anyone."

I sat down at a card table and began cutting the bottoms off the stems at an angle. The flowers get more water that way, so they stay fresh longer. I knew that's what had to be done because Mom had shown me one time when I visited her at Jared's. I also knew Mom and Carol weren't going to have time to do the arrangements right away. Pigsy fell asleep at my feet as I happily snipped stems and re-placed the flowers in the buckets.

A little while later Mom came in. At first I thought she was going to be mad at me, but then she smiled. "That's a good job for you, Sherri. Thank you."

"You're welcome. And see how well Pigsy is behaving," I added.

Mom looked down at the sleeping pig for a long time. "I see," she said. "Just keep it that way."

For awhile things went well. I snipped and Pigsy snoozed. I started thinking about other things I might be able to do that wouldn't get either of us in trouble. I figured I could tie the bows on the swans or count the plates and napkins. I was so busy thinking and snipping that I didn't hear Carol come in.

"Mom says you're doing a great job of keeping the flowers fresh," Carol said as she entered the room.

I looked up and smiled. "I told you I could help," I began, but the expression on Carol's face stopped my words in my throat.

"Sherri, how could you?" she yelled.

"What? What did I do?"

"Not you. That pig!"

"But P.W. is right here sleeping," I said, looking down at my feet. "Uh-oh."

Carol raced over to the buckets of carnations and hauled Pigsy away from one by his leash. "'Uh-oh' is right!" she yelled. "What's the good of keeping a leash on this animal if you don't tie him up? Your precious piece of pork has eaten practically an entire bucket of my wedding flowers!"

That's when I remembered that I hadn't fed Pigsy his pig chow . Just a few grapes and that salad in the kitchen hadn't been enough. I looked at the bucket of half-eaten flowers and shook my finger at Pigsy. "Bad pig!" I scolded.

"A lot of good *that's* going to do," Carol yelled. "Now I have to go to the florist and buy more flowers. They probably won't be able to dye them the same color, and the color scheme will be ruined and..."

Carol paced around the room, pulling at her hair and yelling at the top of her voice. "Everything is going wrong! Get out of here and take that pig with you! You... the pig... you've both given me a migraine headache!"

Carol put her hand to her forehead as I marched stiffly past her. I wondered why she couldn't talk in a normal tone of voice anymore.

Suddenly, Carol's fiancé poked his head in the room. "Hello, everybody," John said, a puzzled grin on his face. "It looks like I came just in time."

I don't know who was happier to see him, me or Carol.

"Oh, John! You came early after all! How wonderful!" Carol gave him a big hug as if I weren't even in the room.

"Hi, Sherri," John said over Carol's shoulder. "Cute pig."

Carol heard what he said and let out a yell that shook the roof. "OUT!" she bellowed at me, and pointed toward the door.

"See you later," John whispered as Pigsy and I passed him. He smiled at me, then winked.

I wasted no more time leaving. I was sure Carol was going to tell John all of the horrible, awful, bad, and nasty things I had done to her. She would say it was my fault that the wedding had so many problems. But I was still glad that John had come early. For one thing, I liked him and knew he would make a great brother-in-law. For another, I thought maybe he could keep Carol from getting any more out of control. *I* sure couldn't!

Nine

PIGSY and I were fooling around in the backyard later that afternoon when John came out to talk.

"The backyard looks nice," he commented, looking around.

"I planted all of the flowers myself," I said, thinking back to when things were still normal. I felt my lips tremble a little, and my eyes got misty. My parents used to count on me to help. I wasn't in the way until Carol came home.

"Why so sad?" John asked. He folded his long legs under him and sat down on the grass next to me. He reached out and gently rubbed

Pigsy's hairy snout.

"Because no one wants me or Pigsy around," I said. "Even if all I'm doing is trying to help, I get yelled at."

"Ten is a tough age," John commented. He plucked a fat blade of grass and blew on it like a whistle. "Here's the call of the flat-footed mallard duck."

"That sounds more like a goose honking," I said, smiling a little.

"Try it," he said. "Put your thumbs on either side so that you have a little opening with the grass straight down the middle. Now blow."

I did as he showed me. At first all I heard was air. I blew harder and harder. Just when I thought my wind was spent, I got a squeak, then a loud squawk.

John chuckled. "Let's play a tune," he suggested. "How about something simple like 'Mary Had a Little Lamb.'"

"How about 'Sherri Had a Little Pig,'" I said.

John nodded and laughed. "Sounds like a

hit to me. Ready, go!"

Together we played the nursery tune on our grass whistles. Of course, it didn't sound anything like a real song. Pigsy perked up his ears to listen. When we were done I rubbed my lips.

"It tickles," I said, finally smiling for real.

"I know," John said. He rubbed his lips too. "And it's such a disgusting sound that it somehow makes you feel better when you're down in the dumps."

That reminded me why I was moping in the backyard. "Carol hates me," I told him. "She's been bugging me all week with her bossy attitude."

"So you started bugging her back," John said. It wasn't really a question.

"She deserves it," I told him. I twirled my blade of grass. Then I tore little bits off the end and stripped off the edges.

"Maybe she does deserve it," John agreed. "What's been happening?"

"Didn't she tell you?"

"Not really. She just went on and on about pigs in the food, pigs on the tables, pigs eating the flower arrangements. She said she was ready to make bacon, lettuce, and tomato sandwiches."

"With Pigsy as the bacon," I said, sighing. "But Pigsy really hasn't been bad. The thing is, everyone starts screaming and it scares him. Like when we came into the living room during the fitting the other day. The seamstress went after him with a yardstick. Wouldn't you run?"

"As fast as my little piggy legs would carry me," John said, laughing. "How did you catch him?"

"I threw a sheet over his head. Only it wasn't a sheet. It was the buffet tablecloth."

"Oh, no," John gasped. His eyes were twinkling, and he couldn't help the laugh that escaped.

"Oh, yes," I said. "And then he sneaked out of my room that night at dinner and licked

Carol's knee under the table. She totally freaked out."

John laughed harder. "And then today he ate the flowers?"

"Not *all* of them," I said. "It's just that he was hungry, which *was* my fault. I should have fed him, but I was so busy making French toast and then cleaning up the kitchen that I forgot. Then I went into the spare room, and he fell asleep while I was working. I didn't notice that he was awake and eating flowers until Carol came in and went berserk."

We both laughed then.

"What's wrong with her, anyway?" I asked John. "When she used to live here, she liked me," I said. "She never bossed me around and told me to get lost."

John stopped laughing and wiped the tears from his eyes. "I guess that putting together this wedding is more of a strain than she thought it would be. Carol is usually very much in control of everything, but this is too much."

P.W. curled up next to me and fell asleep with his head on my lap. I patted his bulging side. I looked up at John. "I still don't see why she has to yell at us."

"No, you don't deserve to be yelled at, and neither does Pigsy," John said softly. "I'll talk to Carol and get her to lighten up, but you need to do your share as well."

"I've been *trying* to help, but they won't let me."

"I'll see if I can fix that, too," John remarked. "But you know that isn't what I mean. What would really help is—"

"I know, I know. Be nicer to Carol," I said with a sigh.

"Exactly. The wedding is only a few days away. I'm sure if you work at it, you can keep from tipping your sister over the edge."

"I'll try," I promised.

"You can start this evening with your fitting," John told me.

"Another fitting?" I cried. "I hate dresses. I

109

hate standing on that stool for hours. I thought they finished with all the fittings the other day."

"Apparently not. The seamstress called when I was on my way out to talk to you and said she would be by at seven o'clock."

"Oh, all right," I said. "I'll stand as still as a statue, and I'll lock Pigsy in my room."

"Oh, there's one more bit of bad news," John said as we stood up together. Pigsy woke up and shook himself.

"What?" I asked.

"Your mom put me in your room tonight because your grandparents are coming and will be using the spare bedroom."

"Where am I supposed to sleep?"

"On the hide-a-bed in the den."

"Why can't I sleep in Carol's room with her?" I asked.

John glanced down at P.W.

"Oh," I said.

"They've already moved your stuff."

"You know, John, I'll be glad when this wedding is over."

"Me, too," he said. "Hey! Want me to make you one of my famous, super-duper root beer floats?"

"Only if P.W. can have some ice cream," I said as we walked into the house, the pig trailing behind.

"Yes, I did hear that Pigsy seems to have quite a craving for ice cream," John said. He laughed and patted Pigsy on the head. "Come on, P.W. You can have as much ice cream as that fat little body of yours can handle."

Ten

LIFE around our house got better after my talk with John and his talk with Carol. She stopped screaming every time I walked past her with the pig. I managed to stand almost patiently while the seamstress made sure my dress fit perfectly.

My grandparents arrived, and things really started happening. At least they wanted me around.

Thursday was the best day of the whole week. I went with Grandpa to rent the chairs and tables we would need for the wedding and reception. Grandma took Lynn and me into my room, and we tied the candy-coated almonds into the net bags. Then we counted out 10 jelly beans for each swan. Mom finished the last of the corsages and took them over to Jared's to keep them cold.

Pigsy didn't bother a soul. He just rooted around in some old newspapers in the den where my bed was made up. When he wasn't doing that, he packed in the food as if he were storing up for winter. He slept a lot, too.

The morning dawned bright and clear on Friday. It looked as if everything was finally falling into place, including the weather. I didn't even really mind sleeping in the den, because I loved having my grandparents around. Grandma took a walk with Pigsy and me Friday morning. And after Grandpa finished wiring an electrical outlet for the band, he found an old sock and played tug-of-war with Pigsy.

"What do you think about this dress?" Grandma asked me later. We had eaten lunch, and Pigsy and I were hanging out in the spare bedroom with Grandma.

"It's pretty," I said. "Is that for the wedding?"

"No, I thought I'd wear it tonight for the re-hearsal. What are you going to wear?"

"I hadn't thought about it. I don't have to wear a dress, do I?"

"It would be nice," Grandma said. "Everyone is going to dress up."

"Oh. But does it have to be a dress?" I asked.

"Not necessarily," Grandma answered. "I didn't like dresses much when I was a young girl, either, but I had to wear them all the time. Come," she said, putting her arm around me and steering me toward my room. "I'll help you find something suitable."

"What about P.W.?" I asked, looking back. Pigsy had fallen asleep by Grandma's suitcase. He had been sleeping all day, except for the short walk and the tug-of-war game.

"Grandpa can take care of him," she said, calling for him.

I felt even better after Grandma helped me

pick out some clothes for the evening. She told me that if I wore a nice blouse and fixed my hair, no one would much care that I was wearing slacks. No one might even notice.

"If you make a big deal of something, then everyone notices," Grandma said. "Sometimes it's just better to quietly go about your business. Things have a way of working out if attention isn't always drawn to them."

"Not always," I said. "When I tried to help all on my own with the flowers, P.W. ate some of them."

Grandma nodded. "I heard about that. But before that happened, you were doing a good job. I'll bet we can find something for you to do today."

"Okay," I said, smiling. "I'm ready."

Grandma and I casually walked into the dining room and set the table for the rehearsal dinner. We made place cards out of paper doilies. We folded napkins into fans, then stuck them upright in the crystal glasses. The table looked really great. I was proud of the job we had done.

Mom and Carol were so surprised and pleased that they let me roll the dough into balls for the dinner rolls—after I had washed my hands three times, of course.

"How's Pigsy?" Carol asked as she filled the mushroom crepes.

Now it was my turn to be surprised. I couldn't believe she was using P.W.'s name in a nice tone. "He's fine," I said. "He's with Grandpa."

"That's good," Carol said, but she didn't sound mad or anything.

Grandma winked at me across the table as we floured our hands and arranged the dough balls in the muffin pans. "See what I mean?" she whispered.

I nodded and winked back. Maybe now that everything was almost done, Carol would start acting like her old self.

It sure seemed like it. I counted at least six

more times that Carol spoke to me without yelling. The rehearsal and dinner went off without a single problem. Pigsy slept almost the whole time.

"Do you think something is wrong with him?" I asked Grandpa at one point. "Can pigs get sleeping sickness?"

"Naw, pigs are just lazy," Grandpa said. "I probably wore him out with that tug-of-war game. He'll be up and around tomorrow."

Then I forgot all about Pigsy because my parents let me stay up late. We played a wild game of cards. While my grandparents and John watched, Carol and I paired off against Mom and Dad. It was just like old times. I was actually beginning to look forward to tomorrow's wedding.

I was bushed when we all finally went to bed. "You know, Pigsy," I said as I changed into a nightgown, "big sisters are okay, I guess, when they're not having a panic fit."

I yawned and slipped under my covers. I

was asleep instantly, dreaming of what a perfect day tomorrow was going to be for a wedding.

* * * * *

Everyone was already up and working when I wandered out to the kitchen at eight o'clock.

"Breakfast is on the counter," Mom said as she hurried past me carrying a flower arrangement. "Grab a bun and a piece of fruit, and then come help us set up the buffet."

"Be right there," I said. I stuffed a warm, sweet hunk of bread in my mouth. "Who made these?" I asked Grandma. She was passing through the kitchen with a silver tray of fancy napkins.

"John did," Grandma answered. "They're good, aren't they? I guess he wasn't able to get much sleep last night," she said. "Wedding jitters, no doubt."

"You're right about that," said John. He was

119

just entering as Grandma was leaving. They smiled at each other. Then John started to dig around in the tool drawer. "So you like my rolls?" he asked.

"Mmm," I said. "They're delicious. You can have jitters more often if it means sweet buns for breakfast."

John laughed and disappeared, a hammer in his hand. He mumbled something about helping the band set up. Some of the band members were friends of his.

I wolfed down my bun, drank a glass of orange juice, and grabbed an apple on my way to help Mom. I could feel the excitement in the air. Everyone was rushing here and there, finishing all of the last-minute details. Carol was fussing over the food arrangements. Mom was putting vases of flowers out. Everyone was trying to keep out of the way of the band members. They were running a last-minute sound check on their instruments.

There was so much to do and so little time

to do it in. I wondered if people would begin arriving before everything was in place. The guests would come and we would all be standing there in our work clothes—flowers, food, and hammers in hand.

Then, somehow, it was done.

Mom glanced at her watch. "The wedding is in less than two hours," she announced. "It's time to start getting dressed. At this point, if something isn't done, just leave it. No one will notice anyway."

John came over to Carol and gave her a big hug. "Are you ready for this?" he asked quietly.

"I don't know if I'm ready for the wedding," Carol said, tapping him playfully on the nose, "but I'm ready to be married to you."

When John dipped his head to kiss her, I grinned and ran off to the den to put on my dress.

I was in my dress and fixing my hair when I heard Carol scream.

What now?

Everyone in the house ran out into the hall to find out what was the matter.

"It's gone!" Carol shrieked. She was wearing a fuzzy, zebra-striped bathrobe. Her hair was in curlers, and she was waving a brush in the air.

John rushed over to her. He must have been in the middle of shaving when Carol screamed. A clump of lather clung to his chin.

"What's gone?" he asked.

Carol pointed her hairbrush directly at me. "My veil! My veil is missing and it's probably that pig's fault!" she yelled.

Uh-oh. It was "pig" again, not Pigsy.

"Why would Pigsy want your veil?" I yelled back. All the good feelings from the last couple of days vanished in a flash.

"He probably ate it," Carol wailed. "What am I going to do? The guests are going to be here any minute and a pig has eaten my veil!"

"Sherri," my mom said in a warning tone.

"Sherri," my dad said in a disappointed tone.

"Don't blame P.W.," I said. "Pigsy is sound asleep in the den by my bed. He has been since yesterday. Come on. I'll show you."

I led the way with Carol, John, my father, my mother, and my grandparents marching along behind me. Poor Pigsy. He had been so worn out and sleepy lately that the shock of seeing seven people would probably freak him out.

"See," I said, pointing to the blanket that I covered him with the night before. "He's still here and there's no veil in sight." I crossed my arms and smiled smugly at Carol.

Then Grandpa reached down and gently pulled the blanket back off of Pigsy. He was gone!

Carol yelled again. "I told you so! I told you so!" she hollered.

"Who stole Pigsy?" I hollered just as loud.

"Why didn't you keep an eye on that pig?"

Mother accused. "This is the most important day of your sister's life and that animal has ruined it."

"I thought we had a deal," John said, frowning. The shaving cream was drying on his chin. He didn't seem to notice. "You promised you wouldn't play any more jokes on your sister."

"But I didn't do it," I said, tears springing to my eyes. "I didn't take the veil or let Pigsy out to get it."

"How do we know?" Carol asked. "You spent all week trying to make me crazy with that pig. Maybe this is your last revenge."

"That's not fair!" I yelled. "All I've done all week is try to help out! You're the one who's acting like a pig!"

Carol balled her hands into fists and stomped toward the door. Grandpa put his hand out to stop her. "Now, listen here everyone. Just because Pigsy and the veil are both missing doesn't mean they're together. If we all search, we're sure to find the pig and the veil."

"Unless that swine has eaten it," Carol said. She burst into tears and raced off.

Mom looked at her watch again. "We have about an hour," she said. "Let's quit standing around and start looking!" She pinned me with a withering look. "I'll deal with you later, Sherri," she said. Her tone of voice meant I was going to be grounded for the rest of my life.

It wasn't fair! I didn't do it.

Frantically, everyone began searching for the veil and P.W. I knew they cared more about the veil, but I was worried about Pigsy. What if someone really had stolen him? What if he had gotten out of the house and was run over by a car? What if he had gotten under the sink in the bathroom and eaten soap? What if he was dead from a bleach overdose and I had to explain to Mrs. Pinkston that I killed her pig?

What if Mom got to him before I did?

A million "what ifs" raced through my head as I dashed from room to room. I was hoping against hope that the missing pig and the missing veil were two separate things. I was also hoping that if they were together, I would be the first one to find them.

Eleven

TIME was running out. We had looked everywhere in the house. No one could find Pigsy or the veil.

Carol and I were the only ones who hadn't given up. We stood looking at each other in the dining room after everyone else went back to their rooms to get ready. "I don't know where else to look," she said. She didn't seem mad anymore, just really tired.

I took a deep breath and let it out in a whoosh. "Pigsy couldn't have gotten out of the house. All the doors were closed last night when we went to bed."

"Wait a minute," Carol said. "John was up

half of the night. He might have gone…outside."

"Uh-oh," I said. "If he did—"

"The storage shed!" we both said together.

We ran through the kitchen to the only place we hadn't looked. The storage shed was just outside the back door to the kitchen. We kept all kinds of things in it, including boxes that contained extra pans for holiday baking. John might have needed a baking pan from the shed when he made his sweet buns.

I got there first. The door was already open a crack. Slowly, I pushed it open all the way. I was just as afraid that Pigsy and the veil would be there as I was that they wouldn't.

At first it was too dark to see anything, and it was as quiet as night. Then I heard a soft sound coming from the corner. I switched on the light and there in the corner of the shed was Pigsy… all wrapped up in Carol's wedding veil.

Carol sank to the floor and burst into a fresh gusher of tears.

"I'm sorry, Carol," I said quietly. "I didn't do it on purpose."

"I know you didn't," Carol said, wiping her eyes and sniffing.

"I'm sorry for all the trouble I caused you all week," I added. "I knew you were flipped out, and I made everything worse by bugging you so much."

Carol sighed. "It wasn't all your fault. I acted like a jerk, too. I shouldn't have tried to do so much, and I should have let you help. But what am I going to do now about my veil?"

"Maybe it's not ripped," I said hopefully, reaching to pull back a corner. "Maybe we can wash it real quick."

But when I uncovered Pigsy we both had a big surprise. Curled up in the folds of Carol's veil were two baby piglets. They were tiny and pink, with tightly closed eyes and scrunched-up noses. Pigsy looked at us and gave a contented little snort.

"You're a *girl* pig!" I exclaimed, reaching out

to stroke Pigsy's head.

"Obviously," Carol said. Then she looked at me and started laughing. "Of all the stories I'll be able to tell my grandchildren," she added when she caught her breath. "I'll bet no one in the history of the world has had piglets born in her wedding veil."

I laughed then, too—but slowly. "You're not mad?" I asked.

Carol sighed. "I'm more mad at myself than at you or Pigsy. I wanted this week to be so perfect. I imagined us all sitting around, talking about old times, wrapping almonds, and having some special family time before the wedding. It didn't work out that way at all. Too many things went wrong. Instead of being relaxed and enjoying my time at home, I went crazy with all of the last-minute stuff."

"Well, there was an awful lot to do," I said.

"Yes, but I went overboard, and I'm sorry, Sherri," Carol said. "I didn't mean to take my frustrations out on you. I guess I just thought

I could be 'superwoman' and do it all."

"You *are* a super woman," I said, meaning it.

Carol smiled. "And you're a super kid sister, Sherri."

Carol and I hugged, and I knew everything was going to be all right.

"Aren't they cute?" Carol said, reaching over to touch a soft, pink, fuzzy ear. "They're so little and helpless. Maybe potbellied pigs aren't such bad pets after all. All things considered, P.W. really *has* been quite tame this week."

"I told you he—*she*—was being good."

"I know," Carol admitted, "but I couldn't see that because I was so caught up in everything else."

"No wonder Pigsy was sleeping so much yesterday," I said, carefully touching the other tiny piglet. "She was getting ready for the big event."

"Speaking of big events," Carol remarked. "I think we'd better get ready for mine. I think P.W. has done all the bothering she's going to do for awhile."

"But what are you going to do about a veil?" I asked.

Carol thought for a moment. Then she leaned down and whispered in my ear. "I've got an idea."

Twenty minutes later we were ready. While the doorbell rang a hundred times, Carol and I dressed together, laughing and joking. Carol fixed my hair, and I buttoned up the back of her dress.

Dad knocked on the door just as we put the finishing touches on Carol's idea. "It's time," Dad said. "Are my girls ready?"

"We're coming," Carol said, winking at me. The music began and Carol took my father's arm. He escorted her through the house to the backyard. It seemed like there were thousands of people, all twisting around to get a look at Carol.

John was waiting at the front, a huge smile on his face. Everyone stood to watch us when the wedding music started. I was the brides-maid, so I went ahead of Carol. I had to admit that even my dress looked great. Everybody took a breath and oohed and aahed as Dad and Carol came down the aisle. Carol looked fan-tastic. Instead of the veil, her hair was woven with baby's breath and peach ribbons. It was perfect, even more beautiful than the veil would have been. Everyone could see Carol's smiling face. Finally, she looked almost relaxed.

Carol really did deserve to have a fantastic wedding. She had worked so hard—we all had. As I watched Carol and John exchange rings, I knew I would remember this moment as one of my happiest.

After the ceremony, we all stayed up at the front, under the archway, to have our pictures taken. The guests started to mingle as we posed for the camera. First Carol and John posed to-gether. Then it was Carol and John and me. Finally, the photographer gathered our whole family together for a group picture.

Carol smiled. John smiled. I smiled. We had done it! Carol and John were married, Carol and I were friends again, and Pigsy was a new mother. How much better could a day go?

"Hold it," the photographer said. "Carol, lay your bouquet in your lap. Now, just let me focus."

Suddenly I heard a squeal from the end of the aisle. Carol heard it too, and we both peered around the photographer to see what was happening.

"Oh, no," Mom groaned.

"Here comes the pig!" John warned.

Startled wedding guests turned to look as Pigsy Wigsy trotted down the aisle. She ran under the photographer's tripod, and over it went. The photographer grabbed for the camera. He caught it just in time, but landed on his knees.

"I can't believe it! It's a pig!" someone shouted loudly.

"Oink alert!" a kid in the front called out.

P.W. ran on, paying no attention. She charged up the steps to the platform we were sitting on, took one look at Carol, and promptly scrambled into her lap. A second later, she was contentedly munching on Carol's bouquet.

I started apologizing before Carol could even think of anything to say. Her mouth just hung open.

"Oh, Carol, I'm so sorry!" I cried. "I never thought... I mean, she was in the shed... I mean, I thought she'd be busy with her babies and..."

Carol looked down at P.W. and then over at me. "Sherri," she said sternly, "I don't think you fed your pig this morning."

"I...I...I... guess I didn't."

"We'll have to remedy that right after the picture," Carol said.

"After the picture?" I asked.

"New mothers need to keep up their strength," Carol said. My mouth dropped open, and I must have looked more surprised than

137

anyone in the audience. I was still waiting for her to blow up at me.

But instead of yelling, Carol started laughing. Then John joined in and so did my parents. Pretty soon the whole audience was laughing too, but I couldn't see what was so funny.

"Why aren't you mad?" I asked.

"Don't you get it, Sherri?" Carol said. "This is the perfect ending to a perfectly silly week. Pigsy has been such a part of this wedding from the beginning that we should have her in the family picture. Take the picture," she instructed the photographer. "I want to remember this moment for the rest of my life."

* * * * *

The reception was in full swing when Mrs. Pinkston arrived. "My flight just came in from London and I came over right away, thinking you'd want Pigsy out from underfoot with all of your guests here," she said. "I don't want to disturb anyone. I'll just take Pigsy and go."

"That may be easier said than done, Mrs. Pinkston," Carol said. "I think Pigsy is kind of attached to our house for a few days."

Mrs. Pinkston raised a questioning eyebrow. "He is?"

I giggled. "We have a little surprise for you," I told her. "Follow me."

I led the way to the storage shed, followed by Mrs. Pinkston and Carol. Mom and Dad came along, too.

We took her over to the corner where Pigsy was busy nursing her piglets. "Pigsy's a girl," I said. "And she wasn't just fat, she was pregnant!"

"Oh, my!" Mrs. Pinkston exclaimed. "Inheriting one pig was interesting, but a whole family? I don't think I'm ready for that! What am I going to do?"

"As a matter of fact," Carol said, "John and I were talking just the other day about getting a pet for our new house. A pig is much quieter than a dog..."

"Would you like one?" Mrs. Pinkston asked. "That would be wonderful. You could have it as soon as it's old enough to be separated from Pigsy Wigsy."

"Carol, I can't believe you actually want a pig for a pet!" I said. "After everything that happened this week?"

"Maybe I want to be reminded of the craziness," Carol said. "I want to remember never to take on too much again. When my life gets too hectic in the future, I'll just stop what I'm doing and play with my pig."

I just shook my head. "But what about the other piglet?" I asked. "Maybe someone here at the wedding would like one? We could ask around."

Mrs. Pinkston smiled. "Well, how about you, Sherri? I can't think of anyone else I'd rather give it to."

"Oh, Mom, Dad, could I?" I asked, turning

to them. My fingers were crossed for luck behind my back.

"We'll see," said Mom. But she and Dad were both smiling. I was pretty sure they would give in.

"Oh boy," I said, hugging everyone in turn. I hugged Carol the hardest and longest—and first. Then I hugged Mom and Dad, and then finally—and carefully—Pigsy Wigsy.

"This has been the best wedding in the history of the world!" I said. P.W. grunted softly and poked her snout into my hand. "You're right," I said to P.W. "It's also the best wedding in the history of pigs!"

About the Author

CINDY SAVAGE lives with her family on a farm in northern California. Cindy has a small, personal zoo of her own, including two cats, Snuggles and Boxer, a ferocious hamster named Frisky Frolic Radical Dude Rock and Roll Savage, and a fish with no name!

When she's not writing books and magazine articles for young people, she likes to spend time with her family, read, do needlework, and bake bread. Some of her other books for Willowisp Press are *The Zoo Crew, Project: Makeover, Caught in the Act, The Curse of Blood Swamp,* and the Forever Friends series.

Cindy loves hearing from the people who read her books. To send her letters, address your envelopes to Cindy Savage, P.O. Box 542, Elk Grove, California, 95624-0542.